AF355495

# SOUNDS IN THE SILENCE

ISBN: 978-93-55462-53-4
eISBN: 978-93-55462-60-2

©Publisher

Publisher: Pharos Books (P) Ltd.
Plot No.-55, Main Mother Dairy Road
Pandav Nagar, East Delhi-110092
Phone: 011-40395855, +14049995474
WhatsApp: +91 8368220032
E-mail: sales@pharosbooks.in
Website: www.pharosbooks.in
First Edition: 2022

Printed By: Sushma Book Binding House, Okhla
Industrial Area, Phase II, New Delhi-110020

**SPUNDS IN THE SILENC**

Smaragdi Mitropoulou

# SOUNDS IN THE SILENCE
Smaragdi Mitropoulou

*a novel*

Translated from Greek by
Dr. Dimitris Thanasoulas

*"…in the old Sanskrit dialect, Ravi means Sun… But now, it had been a while that the sun had set…"*

# CONTENTS

# *Introduction*

"Let silence be blessed! Because once you are in it, you will hear me speak"
(Kahlil Gibran).

In the book "Sounds in the Silence," Smaragdi Mitropoulou's lyrical and elegant writing cannot leave the reader unmoved.
Like the lyrics from **Song of Marisol**
**Once the sea was filled with blood,**
**The roses stopped blooming...**
**Only one was left...**
**On the finger**
**And the heart as a mark.**

In her collection of short stories, major themes are the love of the sea, the haunted past, the dreams that smell of jasmine, the bittersweet memories, the repentance that births redemption and finally the intimidating hereafter.

The glossy recording of everyday life and the intense poetic element without foggy expressions are distinct throughout this work.

Most of the stories are set against the backdrop of the sea and the Greek islands' chapels. The black-and-white photographs and the chests full of memories take us on a journey to another world, that of Smaragdi Mitropoulou, where the blue of the sky and the red of love and affection embrace the whole creation. They transfer us to island neighbourhoods and deserted beaches. They throw us into the "forty waves," hiding Poseidon between the lines. They light fires next to the boats, where some people give their first erotic kiss.

Her heroes are ordinary people, usually rural. People who talk in whispers and, through silence, acquire a sharp echo. Entities in a meteoric step from the turbulent past to a redemptive future. Souls who seek serenity and the light.

In the last part of the book, there's a chapter with her poems. Its title is "The Lyrics of My Heart."

They're four poems with the following titles: **Silence, Rain, Anticipation, Let There Be Light.** The titles are in the absolute and correct chronological order and have a great theological resonance.

From the silence, therefore the inexistence, 1st poem
To the rain, therefore the creation, 2nd poem
To the anticipation, therefore the hopeful waiting, 3rd poem
To the light, our final destination, 4th poem.
And so, she poetically creates a theological circle of life.

Smaragdi Mitropoulou's poetry is primarily erotic, but also symbolic and romantic. Memory has the primacy. The poetic discourse turns backwards and inwards, addresses the past and belongs to its territory. Pessimism, melancholy, sorrow, unfulfilled love, loss, and nostalgia are its main themes.

It negotiates, among other things, love and its memory, separation, and the capture of accomplished beauty. Lastly, the sea, the earth, the moon, light, and darkness are archetypal symbols that function as "associative complexes."

*Theofanis L. Panagiotopoulos,*
*theologian, poet, writer, and radio producer.*

### *Voices*

*Ideal and beloved voices*
*of those who are dead, or of those*
*who are lost to us like the dead.*

*Sometimes they speak to us in our dreams;*
*sometimes in thought the mind hears them.*

*And with their sound for a moment return*
*other sounds from the first poetry of our life --*
*like distant music that dies off in the night.*

*C.P. Cavafy, Poems, Volume 1, Ikaros Editions.*

# Part One
## Sea, Expatriation, and Love
## And a Life that Seems More
## Like a Fairytale.


### Song of the Sea

*Ah! Foreign lands draw happiness*
*From my sweet-smelling flower,*
*My flesh and blood.*[1]

A song covered by the haze of time, or so he thought. It stayed hidden in a corner of his heart to bring to mind his noble island… during his hours of loneliness *"in foreign and distant places."*

And it was as if Anastasis could see his mother in front of him, the captainess singing it, sitting by her window with the embroidery in her hand.

Built on the rock, their home gazed at the vast deep blue. So many times, she looked with mixed emotions at the sea… the sea that had taken her man, her captain, the skipper of her heart, and had jealously imprisoned him in her own arms.

And then…

"I'll write to you, mother, you'll see, my absence won't be for long," he had promised her shortly before boarding the ship.

"Godspeed, my beloved!"

She wasn't tearful, but inside, her heart must have been broken into many pieces.

Beside her, teary-eyed, Marousso, *Maroussaki* – as he called her – his first love. The tender intertwining of their fingers and that look of hers, full of pain and love, was the last image he took with him and inside him.

"And as long as you remember, you're still alive!" he said to himself.

The first thing he saw from the large veranda of his father's home was a small white church with a blue roof, dedicated to Panagia Thalassini, the Virgin Mary of the Sea. His parents were married there and he had sworn to make Marousso his wife there too.

---

[1] Traditional folk song.

Nearly twenty years had passed.

*Damn you, expatriation…*

He had missed and longed so much for the aura of his island.

****

The old town with the mansions, the bougainvillea and the jasmines seemed to hover between earth and sky.

He couldn't hold back his tears as – at last! – he returned to his fairy state.

*"You're a fairy, and I'm the king in our fairy state,"* he said to his Maroussaki.

"My mother, my soul, my love and my Panagia Thalassini," he whispered, facing the church bell tower.

He was only a few steps away.

Cooped up in his paternal home for a long time, she patiently waited for him.

As he opened the iron door, a scent of jasmine mixed with sea and saltiness hit his nostrils.

"My flesh and blood!" he heard or thought he heard his mother's voice.

*Are my ears playing tricks on me?* he wondered.

Mother had now moved to another mansion, somewhere in heaven. From there, she prayed for her Anastasis to return and give life to dead dreams and hopes.

"My flesh and blood!" he heard again, more clearly this time.

"Marousso!" he exclaimed in surprise.

He wanted to tell her and ask her so much. A glance at her right hand made him understand a lot.

The ring he had once given her, with the scars of time on it, she hadn't let go of it.

*"I'll wait for you for a lifetime,"* she had told him then.

"I've been waiting for you! I would, even if it took a lifetime!" she told him again now.

She gently pulled him inside.

In the dining room, the framed photo with the fresh flowers next to it seemed to welcome him.

"I didn't have time… then… I didn't…," he said and burst into tears.

Marousso opened her arms and he nestled in there like a child.

"What fairytale and song do you want me to tell you, so that you don't cry, my flesh and blood?" she told him tenderly.

Ah, these words of hers, mixed with the mother's voice!

He raised his head and wiped his eyes with the back of his hand.

"No more fairytales! I want us to live, my soul, live! It's not too late for us, is it, my Maroussaki?" He stared at her anxiously, waiting for her answer.

The bell of Panagia Thalassini, which rang for the vespers, interrupted their conversation.

"In a few days, it's Her Grace's celebration," said Marousso and did the sign of the cross.

They looked at each other in silence for a while.

"On Her grace's Day, you'll be my wife!" said Anastasis and hugged her by the shoulders.

The bougainvillea leaves next to them moved slightly.

"You have my blessing, my flesh and blood!" The blast of wind and the captainess's voice were balm for both their hearts.

Marousso caressed his cheek.

"Yes, my dear, yes!" she told him. "Time for us to live too!"

## *Grandma's Treasure*

Once upon a time, in a big village in Arcadia, lived a sweet old lady, in a wooden two-storey house… she loved her grandchildren and told them the most beautiful fairytales.

Her name was *Smaragda*, but her fellow villagers called her *Mrs. Dimitraina*, from her deceased husband's name.

Her loved ones called her Smaragdenia.

Grandma never made distinctions among her children and grandchildren. I, however, had a special bond with her because we shared the same name.

Since I can remember myself, I spent the summers by her side, in the village.

A carved walnut chest in her bedroom always aroused my curiosity.

As a child, I liked making up stories about its content.

"It has a treasure! The good fairy gave it to Grandpa, because he saved her from the bad dragon!" I said.

"What good fairy?" the grownups asked me, probably having fun with my naivety.

"The one who lives in the great spring… at the entrance of our village, of course!" I responded with grit.

Growing up, my interest in Grandma's chest started to fall to second place. First, came studies, master's degrees abroad, and then chasing a career and the various obligations.

As for the chest, it stayed forgotten in Grandma's room, together with her fairytales, buried in a corner of my mind.

Who had time for all that? I had now landed in the adults' world.

At least, I believed so.

How long had it been, really, since I last visited my little homeland?

It was Grandma's death that brought me back again!

She died *old and full of days*, as we say, but I felt like a part of me was lost along with her, maybe the one that kept living pure and unadulterated somewhere in the depths of my soul.

In her handwritten will – closed and sealed, *"until that time comes,"* in an envelope in her commode's first drawer in the dining room, there was – among other things! – a detail about me.

The chest of my childhood would become mine.

I smiled.

That little girl from the innermost depths of my being began to reemerge to the surface.

And while the rest of the family had left the village, I preferred to stay at the old house and spend my night *"in my grandmother's room."*

I sat on the edge of the bed and stroked the rainbow-coloured woolen knitted blanket.

*How much I once liked to roll over it,* I thought.

I put my hand under the pillow and pulled a long rusty key. I took a deep breath and…

*"My little Smaragdenia, this is my treasure!"* I heard a gentle whisper.

Touching the chest and its contents, I felt like I was becoming little Smaragdenia again, longing for her grandmother's caresses and fairytales and looking forward to discovering the hidden treasure.

I caught in my hands a traditional parure with three rows of silver coins. *"When the girls in the village got married, my sweetheart, they wore a parure around their necks with lots and lots of coins,"* my grandmother often told me. With the eyes of my soul, I imagined her wearing it on her wedding day and shining all over.

Next to the parure, there was the silver buckle,[2] that I saw her put on with her good costume *"on the big days and the holidays."* It had roses carved on it and in the middle two doves kissing.

*"We lived like two little pigeons with your grandfather Dimitros, my dear…"*

I placed the parure and the buckle carefully on the bed and began to look at a gold-embroidered *fermeli*[3] and two gold-plated revolvers.

*"These belonged to your distant great-grandmother…"*

I had heard the story of Arkadiani several times: *"a girl like fresh water… and with a soul of steel… when the Turks were headed here… she cut her long hair… put on a masculine attire… girded with weapons… and went out into the mountains with the klephts…"*

*Who saw a fish on the shore, the sea sown?*
*Who saw a beautiful girl dressed as a klepht?*

---

[2] Buckle on women's clothing.

[3] A white woollen jacket.

Grandma's favourite song came back to my mind.

I wiped a salty drop that rolled imperceptibly, and I continued the search. I discovered a medal and a diploma.

The medal was quite worn… I could, however, distinguish the engraved date: 1922.

*Honourable mention…* I could barely read the faded letters on the paper.

Grandpa's medal of bravery and accolade! They had been awarded to him for his exploits on the Asia Minor Front!

A little further down, I found his letters to Grandma… yellowed and time-worn, they hid so much love in them.

*"My beloved Smaragdenia…"* they all started.

*"Light the candle to the Virgin Mary and pray that I will come out of this fire alive. And when, God willing, I come back to you, we'll have a wedding that the village will remember for years…"*

*"Did the flowers bloom in your yard, my heart? Did the vine grow?*
*I'm dying to get to see you again, my heart,*
*To be crowned with the vine in your yard."*

I put them back in place and opened a small wooden box full of old photos and dried lavender leaves.

Grandma and Grandpa's wedding photo… my father and uncles still kids… and other relatives, close and distant.

An entire lifetime hidden in a chest!

The most wonderful fairytale was unfolding in front of me. It didn't talk about princesses, princes, dragons, or fairies, but about the beauty of life, the joy that is often hidden in the small, simple things.

And Grandma Smaragdenia was always my good fairy.

The dawn found me awake.

I got up, poured some water on my face and dialed a number on my cellphone.

"Hello?"

"I don't want us to sell the house in the village, father!"

"But my girl…"

"How can we sell our soul, huh? We will revive it from the start!"

There was a muffled sob and a whispered *"thank you, my child,"* as the line hung.

I made a cup of coffee on the embers and sat in the rocking chair by the window to watch the sunrise.

Thousands of shades of gold and blue flooded the sky and my soul along with it.

"Good morning, beginning of my own fairy tale," I said out loud and smiled.

# *Part Two*
### *As the sounds sing in silence,*
### *they know how to whisper*
### *a thousand "I love you's."*

### *Sounds in the Silence*

*Time to give life to those words that persistently dance within you. I will be holding your hand and lead it. For your love… for my love… for the hours of silence. Because I've walked on and will walk on only with you.*
*As the sounds sing in silence,*
*They know how to whisper a thousand "I love you's."*

He looked at the sea. It spread under her feet like melted silver under the moonglow. She stroked the bunch of wildflowers she was holding in her hands, kissed their petals, and with a sudden movement, threw them into the waves.

"Farewell!" she whispered. "Farewell!"

For several weeks now, Margarita had been following the same ritual. At night… those cold, wet winter nights, when all the island's inhabitants stayed home, she slipped from the alleys, like a ghost, went up the path that led to the area of the big rock and…

Always at the same time. At midnight. In silence… only the sound of the monastery bell interrupted her, whenever it tolled for some overnight procession.

Just like tonight.

****

The flames of the funeral pyre rise to the sky, and I see them wrapping in their arms my most beloved man, my father. For everyone else, he was Ravi, the painter of silence. For me, he was the truest, most essential part of my life. A little further, my mother tries to hide her pain behind a pair of dark glasses. Even though she was divorced from my father when I was a teenager, she always held a special place in her heart. During his sick days – when his disease gradually stole his breath… his voice… – she stood by his side… until the last moment… a moment long enough to hurt her!

****

"Ravi!" stuttered Margarita and knelt on the ground.

In the old Sanskrit dialect,[4] Ravi means Sun. But now, it had been a while that the sun had set.

Midnight… already midnight.

"Ravi!" she uttered again.

****

Midnight.

My mother is withdrawn to her old bedroom. She wants to be alone with her memories; that's what she told me.

With trembling hands, I put the key in the keylock of the *"hidden room."* *"Hidden"* since my father wouldn't let any of us in there, as long as he was alive.

It was his refuge during his hours of silence, a silence that had now become his constant companion. Only painting gave him a tiny spark of smile.

Or maybe not?

Time to find out his hidden secrets.

****

Until now, Margarita had managed to keep her secret. Maybe anyone who saw her, anyone who learned, would say that she spent her life for a lie, for a shadow.

She shuddered at the thought.

"It was… it was… like a dream… but it wasn't a lie… it was not a lie," she said aloud.

****

Now, that's a surprise… paintings depicting the same person in different poses!

A woman.

______________

[4] India's classical language.

Only the scenery remains the same: a large rock and all around the blue of the sea and the sky.

At the table by the window, a blue folder catches my eye.

*What role did this colour play in your life, father?* I wonder opening it.

Sheets of paper, filled with his calligraphic writing.

A small envelope with a name written on the outside: Margarita. And inside, photos… of the woman in his paintings.

*"To you… to you… to you,"* the same dedication to all.

********

Margarita let her tears run freely.

It's the moment when the pain doesn't just reach its limits but surpasses them and seeks a way out to spurt like an impetuous river… there, on the big rock, where earth, sea, and sky become one.

********

I reverently touch the papers…

*A flower was born tonight…* I read, with a voice broken by emotion.

*I would like to run and roll in a vast meadow of daisies…*

*I would like to sing that – yes! – the daisy opened its petals… it received the sun in it.*

*Hold me in your arms… make me yours… don't let me get lost…*

*(………)*

*I speak to you through the language of my silence. And I tell you a thousand words…*
*MY LOVE… MY LOVE… MY LOVE…*

*(………)*

*Yes, I know… I know that you crave me the same… the nights when the body wriggles and trembles from loneliness and lack… in crumpled and wet sheets…*

*(………)*

*My only joy is your letters… my only company is your photos…*

*(………)*

*That strange red-haired gypsy, I remember, had told me: "For you, love will come beyond the sea. But… but… only through colours, words on paper and silences will you be able to touch it… to feel it… when only the sounds in silence will speak…"*

*(.........)*

*And if I never see you with the earthly eyes… I will see you with the eyes of the soul…*

*(.........)*

*I will come to meet you… all the signs lead where heaven and earth… heaven and sea meet…*

*(...........)*

*Margarita: I only need that word… only that word… I only need you… you… to say goodbye to the world… at the time of silence…*

****

Midnight.

The time when what is hidden begins to come out to the light.

Midnight.

The time that a soul has chosen to go to beloved places.

Midnight.

The time when a bunch of wildflowers travels in the sea waves.

Midnight.

The time when the sounds in silence play their own invisible melody.

****

*"It was… it was… like a dream… but it wasn't a lie… it was not a lie," your words are engraved in me, Margarita.*

*You can't see me. But I've been by your side for a long time now. I follow you. I hug you in your dreams.*

*At that strange mysterious hour, as the veil that separated yesterday from tomorrow and the present from the eternal was torn, I refused to climb the steps of the stars.*

*And I forever stayed there… between land, sea and sky.*

*For your love… for my love… for the hours of silence.*

*Even though I never saw you… even though I never touched you… even though I never tasted you.*

*When midnight strikes.*

# Part Three
## How can memories fool time?


## Ingratitude

As the light of dawn fought the darkness of the night, a noise was heard, at first lowly, almost dimly, and then more intensely, something like a roar and a painful scream, disturbing the calm of the island. And as time went on, it became stronger and stronger, making its presence more and more noticeable.

The howling of the wind together with that of the sea.

The house near the rocks was surrounded by the wind's impetus, which swept everything in its path. Mercilessly, it broke the branches and scattered on the ground the buds of the lemon tree, – which lordly dominated the garden, poor thing! – turned over the flowerbeds with the roses, furiously uprooted the gardenias, plucked them, and dragged their flowers down to the sea.

The sky was filled with black, leaden clouds and between them faintly appeared a bloody scarlet moon.

*It smells like death,* many people thought.

****

She got up from the little escritoire,[5] opened the curtain and looked at the flurry outside.

"That's how my soul has been for so many years!" she said softly and crossed herself.

She sat back on the chair, took the pencil in her hand and continued writing.

She wrote… she wrote… she wrote as if she was in a hurry to finish everything tonight… as much as her time-worn hands allowed her, of course.

A loud noise made her get up again with difficulty and approach the glass.

*God Almighty!* she thought.

------

[5] A small writing desk.

The waves, reinforced by the wind, get wilder, inflated, and hit the rocks hard, reaching the small house's yard. If it were possible, they'd surely tear it down.

"It's cold…" she monologued.

She sat in her armchair, wrapped herself in a red knitted blanket and closed her eyes.

Suddenly, the window slammed open.

And everything went dark.

****

The first ray of sunshine that shone timidly looked around in sadness.

It caressed the crumpled, bloody, dismembered flowers with affection. Some of their sad relics were visible on the surface of the water, along with some sheets of paper, written in ink.

The word *INGRATITUDE* was barely readable.

The other words were soaked and dissolved.

It was destined only for the sea to learn about the one and only love of that woman who however was forced to renounce it because, after her parents' death, she was the only guardian and protector of three minor brothers.

He left; he returned to his hometown, in pain from her rejection.

She stood by the little ones, like a mother and a father; she worked wherever she could so that they have everything they need. She took care of their education and their settlement.

Until she got 50 years old, when her brothers had long spread their own wings, a telegram informed her about *his* death.

So, she left her place and came to his place, the little secluded island, to be – even like this – near him, to light the candle at his tombstone and bring to him roses and gardenias.

*"The most beautiful for you, with the first kiss of dawn,"* she said.

And time went by, and one season succeeded the other. Her siblings – absorbed in their own lives! – had almost forgotten about her. Not a single phone call, not a single letter.

Only once did one of her brothers call her *"for an emergency,"* as he said. And his voice was almost cold, distant. She listened to him silently and, while he was talking, she silently hung up the phone.

"*How much ingratitude can one* take!" were the only words she said.

And then, she began to fill sheets of paper with the pain in her heart… these sheets that were now slowly dissolving.

The sunbeam warmed the sleeping woman's frozen face. Where she travelled, no bitterness or ingratitude could touch her anymore.

Outside, a little white bud from the once lush gardenia and a red bud from the rose next to it were left forsaken and half-buried in the sand.

# *How Much Do Memories Hurt?*

### 1

Alekos hadn't set foot in Kypseli, Athens, in thirty-five years. After that fateful night, he burned his boats and never looked back. He built his life all over on the other side of the Atlantic, in New York. The struggle, the moil, and time, this ruthless enemy of every human being, distanced him from everyone and everything, even from his childhood friend, Vangelis.

Kypseli Square had changed; it had nothing to do with back when, with the time of his youth.

"Do you remember?" Vangelis asked him, as they were walking in their old whereabouts.

Alekos shook his head.

What was left? Nothing but memories.

In the place of the club where couples of lovebirds used to rock embraced to sounds of blues, holding a glass of vermouth, a block of flats of questionable quality had now sprouted. Its occupants were dark-skinned, almost black, wore strange, colourful clothes and spoke a different language.

"Oh Miranda," slipped out of his mouth.

*How did I remember her?* he thought. *Miranda... with her long black hair, the curly eyelashes and super mini dresses. Kinda like Elena Nathanail! A fully feminine female.*

Vangelis frowned.

*Miranda... Miranda...* he thought. *The most beautiful girl in the world... Miranda.*

In a strange way, they were both fascinated by that girl. As for her, she wanted so much to experiment.

How is it to have two young men longing for you? Sharing you? "Doing" you at the same time?

And you... you are... throbbing, melting, crawling, and soaring? Feeling their sighs, moans, and groans?

### 2

It all started at night and ended just before dawn, at the KYPSELI hotel, on a side street of Fokionos Negri. Room number 13, decorated in deep red colour: carpet, wallpaper, covers on the double bed.

Alekos wanted to be "her first." Always. He demanded that she wear black lingerie with red lace. These colours stimulated him, turned him on.

*"Black as darkness, red as* fire," he used to say.

He didn't kiss her. Thirsty and insatiable, he hugged her passionately, tore her underwear with one movement and penetrated her with force while holding her glued down with his hands… Other times he turned her face down and…

Their union was fierce, without tenderness, almost animalistic… it ended with loud groans.

Vangelis caressed her all over, in her most secret places, with his hands, with his tongue, filled her with kisses with his lips. Her breath was getting increasingly sharp and loud, as if telling him, *"come on! come on…!"* and then he gently took her, made her numb, but also explode, whispering sweet nothings in her ear. And Miranda sighed and mixed her hot breath with his, her sweat with his sweat, her juices with his juices.

*Each in their own way,* thought Vangelis. *Although I…*

Although he had begun to fall in love with her and want her to become his, only his. And while until then the peculiar trio seemed to be having a good time, Vangelis started feeling the first stings of jealousy.

*"We had agreed to share everything; that was our deal," Alekos had reminded him in a discussion.*

*"Yes… but…"*

*"Remember the bet we made. We won it, didn't we? Why do you want to spoil it now? Aren't we having fun, all three of us? And Miranda, you see it… don't you see it? That little whore is aroused by the both of us…"*

*"But… perhaps…"*

*"She wants us to screw her, you idiot. Both me and you. If you caress her, that's another thing. That will turn her off, and then the birdie will fly away. She just wants a hard fuck. If you so much as talk to her about love and affection, she will send you back to where you came from… wake uuuuup…"*

"The KYPSELI hotel has been ruined," sighed Alekos. "Who knows what kinds of junkies and bums find shelter there at night!"

"How many memories," reminisced Vangelis. "Nights full of passion, eh? Ah, Miranda!"

"Damn!" roared Alekos through his teeth.

3

They stood short.

"Back then… here… do you remember?" Vangelis asked his friend.

Alekos shook his head.

*For how long, I wonder? How much longer?* he thought.

Past.

*That night, he had gone out for a lonely walk in Fokionos Negri. An ugly premonition had been consuming him since noon. He was afraid that something was going to happen. It was as if he didn't know where he was going. Those hangouts seemed so familiar to him, but also so unknown at the same time.*

*His footsteps led him to a small thicket a little down the road. He heard whispering voices behind a tree.*

*"But I love you, Miranda. Don't you believe me?"*

*It was the voice of his friend, Vangelis.*

*"I like you too… you are so… so different… sweet… amazing…"*

*Alekos clenched his fists.*

*"The other guy… only wants one thing: to 'take' me in any way… and… I'm… I liked it in the beginning but now… now I hate it," Miranda continued.*

*He didn't need to hear anything more. With a leap, he got in front of them.*

*"Is that so, you traitor?" he thundered at his friend. "We'd share everything; isn't that what we had agreed? To share everything… everything. Even this whore right here! What has changed now, huh? What changed?"*

*"I told you I was starting to have feelings for her," Vangelis defended himself, trying to look calm. "But no… you didn't… you wouldn't listen. All you cared about was the bet… A silly bet… when we were half-drunk…"*

*"Alekos, I… we…" Miranda intervened.*

*"You what, huh? You what? You whore…"*

*The slap on her cheek resounded like a thud.*

*"Nooo!" Vangelis tried to get in the middle, but Alekos, with his stronger upper body, pushed him aside.*

*"Bitch! Everything was fine when I fucked you… and now…"*

*Miranda opened her mouth to say something, but a loud blow made her nose bleed.*

*"Alekos!" she said complainingly, almost beggingly.*

*Beside himself with anger, he rushed at her and grabbed her by the throat.*

*"Let her go!" screamed Vangelis, trying with all his might to pull his friend's hands away from Miranda.*

*Alekos, however, couldn't hear neither Vangelis… nor the unfortunate girl's muffled cries, as she struggled in vain to breathe. His fingers clenched more… and more…*

*As if in a dream, he saw Miranda leaning on him with her eyes wide open and then falling down.*

*"What did you do? What have we done?" Vangelis' voice was heard.*

*Alekos stood motionless, speechless.*

*Vangelis knelt on the ground and bent over Miranda.*

*"Girl… talk to us… he didn't want to do this… we didn't mean to. Sorry…" he kept repeating, giving her light slaps on the face.*

*Inside, however, he knew it was in vain.*

*Miranda was no longer here.*

*"Oh, my God!" he gasped again. "What did you do? What have we done to her?"*

*Alekos did not answer. He just grabbed his friend by the hand, and they started running, running, running.*

"I'm sick…" Alekos broke the silence. "Doctors give me a maximum of three months…"

"But you lived. You lived. While she…"

Alekos looked his friend in the eyes.

He only uttered, "Did I live?"

4

*Ah, these memories… how much they hurt,* Alekos thought, as if he were left alone.

And it wasn't the first time he had had this thought.

He served himself a double whiskey and went out on his hotel room's balcony. The city lights unfolded before him like a colourful carpet. This is how he enjoyed the view of New York from his flat's large window.

"Did I live, really?" he wondered.

There were times when the darkness of night made him shudder. He put on music to break the strange feeling that "something" was around him: in his mind, in his body, on the four walls of his house.

A strange invisible presence… that became particularly intense whenever he tried to create a relationship.

Women who warmed his lonely nights left him at the first light of day and never wanted to see him again.

He knew but didn't dare to admit it.

It was *her.*

What did she want? Did she want to remind him of the life, youth and dreams he deprived her of? Or…

He looked up at the sky, slowly sipping his drink. The moon seemed to be playing hide-and-seek with a cloud: it hid for a while, then appeared again.

Alekos flounced, feeling "something" on his shoulder. Upset, he glanced to the side. It was a branch of greenery from the pot.

"Phew!" he exhaled with relief.

*Full moon tonight,* he thought and was about to smile.

He stood mid-smiling when he saw gloom slowly covering the square. The city lights, which shone before, were now starting to look dim.

"You've grown old, my friend, you can no longer stand alcohol," he monologued.

He entered the room and left the glass on the nightstand.

And then…

"Something" like a caress touched his cheek. A frozen caress. In the semi-darkness… he thought he saw an elusive shadow. The curtain rustled slightly.

*What kind of games is my imagination playing tonight? It can't be… no…. no… I'm dazed by the alcohol…* he thought.

He turned on the main light and sat on his bed. His forehead and arms were soaked in sweat; he was almost shaking.

"I've been waiting for you," he heard a voice whisper in his ear.

A female voice.

A voice he knew well.

"Miranda!" he shouted and jumped up.

*Come… come…* he heard again.

"What do you want from me? I was… I was crazy then… full of jealousy… I considered everything I touched my property… even you… even….!

There's only me to blame… Only me… and my obsessions… my stupid obsessions! That's why I'm paying… paying every day… for years now… I'm paying."

*Even so, you lived!* the same voice. *While I…*

"Lived? You think I lived? Well, no! No, no! I didn't live, Miranda, I didn't live… It's you, everywhere and always…. You are everywhere and always…"

Another touch on his back and at the base of his neck.

*The love you didn't give me…* he heard.

"The love I didn't give you…" he repeated like an echo.

Frozen lips joined his. A ravenous, passionate kiss that smelled of evening primrose and soil.

*Life… breath… my breath…*

"Mi… Miranda… l… o… v… e… me!"

****

Vangelis put the flower he was holding on the marble.

"Godspeed, Alekos, my old friend!" he wished.

A few days ago – when he went to visit him – he had found him dead, with his shirt unbuttoned.

"Heart attack!" said the official report.

When closing his friend's eyes, only Vangelis noticed a tiny fresh mark of red lips on Alekos's neck. Once, his body too was full of the exact same hot marks… once…

A strange scent of primrose wafted in the air.

"The circle is closing," he whispered, sighing. "Did you forgive me, Miranda?" "How much the memories hurt me now!"

## *Marisol's Song*

*When the sea was filled with blood,*
*The roses stopped blooming…*
*Only one was left…*
*A mark on the finger and the heart…*

He put aside the pencil and closed the blue half-worn notebook.

It was getting dark.

Only one word rose to his lips: *Marisol.*

He touched the long chain hanging around his neck. He always wore it hidden underneath his shirt, as if he wanted to keep a secret.

After a long absence, he was again on the sacred island.

"Like today…" he repeated softly.

Every year on this day, he had the same thoughts… thoughts that hurt him… but now, they were more intense.

He knelt before the small old icon of the Virgin Mary – *"his consolation and confessor"* and hid his face in his palms.

*The road is long,* he thought. *Only You know the truth… only You… that hear me without judging me.*

****

He wasn't always Brother Raphael with the permanently sad – as if ready to weep – look.

He was once called Spyros. Everyone admired him for his powerful mind and "mathematical" thinking. It was no coincidence that, as a teenager, he had won three medals at Mathematical Olympiads. What could be more natural than not only studying this science but also continuing his studies at a higher level abroad?

And then, he was appointed to an island in the Dodecanese, a small but blessed one. And he loved every corner of it… every inch… the scent of its flowers… the waves of its sea.

In that place, Patmos, he discovered his aptitude for poetry. So, he filled entire notebooks which remained locked in his desk's drawer.

In a building struggling with the wear and tear of time, he tried, in addition to mathematical symbols and formulas, to teach children to dare to dream.

No woman had been able to unlock his heart. Aside from a couple of frivolous relationships, he remained single during his studies.

When night fell, he dreamed of *the girl who* would become his other half, his destiny. Like we said, apart from a mathematician, Spyros was also a poet. And poets often resort to a fairytale world.

*Nights full of fragrant roses*

*Sounds of castanets and flamenco guitar,*

*Lips meeting under the moonlight…*

How had he come up with these verses, really?

In a two-storey old mansion, a little farther from the Monastery of Theologos, his fate winked at him.

And Spyros got caught in love's webs.

Her name was Marisol, and she was from Granada… the fruit of the marriage between a Greek woman from the holy island and a Spanish singer who had come for a concert. And now, the wave had brought her to her mother's old paternal home to find a shelter. She turned the lower floor into an atelier where she spent several hours painting and making jewellery. In the garden, she planted red rose bushes.

She wore a silver ring with a red rose-shaped stone… and never parted it.

She loved the music of her homeland and so, the sounds of flamenco were mixed with the sound of the monastery bell.

*My desire for you dear*

*looks like the vast gardens*

*in the palaces of Granada.*

*Desire and pain together,*

*love and tear.*

Now, Spyros's poems were addressed to the fairy of his heart. Their nights were filled with aromas, music, kisses, and promises.

*Nights full of fragrant roses*

*Lips that meet under the moonlight…*

*Lady of my heart, for you I took the guitar in my hands,*

*Lady of my heart, for you I will sing…*

They say that gods envy people's happiness!

****

"Hey, lad!" An affectionate voice brought him back to the present. "Master Emilianos!"

Two warm hands held him tight.

Emilianos, his old schoolmaster, the Master, as everyone called him.

"How many years!" exclaimed Brother Raphael.

"You left and didn't look back, my Spyros! I never understood that decision of yours… never…"

"Please… please… don't…"

Emilianos dry-coughed.

"He's very bad… we must hurry…"

****

The man's body appeared emaciated under the covers. His face was pale as a sheet. As soon as Brother Raphael entered the room, he cast his hazy gaze on him.

"Y… you… came…"

"My boy… yes… I'm here…"

The sick man stretched out his scrawny hand.

"I get scared… when dark falls, I get scared…"

He leaned on the pillow, raddled. Brother Raphael stroked his forehead.

"A big lie… a big lie… if you knew…"

****

Like a bird, time travels to the past.

Alexis, a young colleague, had come to the school that year. A teacher of Byzantine music, raised on strict principles, he believed that *"in life, we must beware of temptation… we need vigilance and prayer… dreams can at some point harm the soul's purity."*

The window of his small cell – in the monastery's guesthouses – looked out on the courtyard of Marisol's house. Early in the morning when he got up to pray, before leaving for school, he watched Marisol water her flowers… at the time of midday rest, her singing resounded in his ears… and at night, he saw the shadows of two naked entangled bodies behind the curtain.

The yellow wet stain on his sheets made his face take on a pale colour, a red deeper than the roses in the Spaniard lady's garden.

*"No, no, I mustn't!"* he kept repeating. *"It's a sin… no… I shouldn't!"*

He didn't dare confess to his own self, let alone to his confessor, that his body was upset and shivering at the thought of Marisol, that his soul bled, that he often watched the couple.

*Prayer is the strongest medicine…* and Alexis prayed and cried, cried and prayed, and whipped his body with a wicker rod to atone for his "sinful" thoughts.

Marisol means Mary of the Sun. But for Alexis, Marisol was the Mary of Fire, the Mary of Temptation, the Mary of Sin.

And the rod kept leaving marks on his back and chest.

****

The sick man wiggled his lips. All that was heard was an imperceptible whisper.

****

They say that gods envy people's happiness!

Apart from her handicrafts, Marisol was also distinguished for her charm and temperament. Most men on the island went by her studio to order gifts for their wives and daughters and heaped praise on her art… and her sweetness and grace.

The Spaniard lady always smiled at them cordially, but her heart and mind were given only to Spyros… who, however, began to throw tantrums almost every day as he felt the clouds of jealousy blurring his mind.

"But how is this possible?" she argued. "Are you blind? Can't you see how much…?"

"All of them are literally undressing you with their eyes… and you enjoy it, don't you?"

"You're unfair. I don't…"

How did he raise his hand and forcefully slap her face?

Marisol swallowed the sob that soared in her throat, caught Spyros by the arm, opened the door and pulled him out.

And since then, her door never reopened for him, no matter how much he cried, no matter how much he begged her.

****

*You were a proud woman, my dear. One of your many gifts that I admired…and adored! But I had regretted, Marisol, I had regretted it. I struggled to show it to you, my love! Ah, damned be that cursed day…," thought Brother Raphael.*

****

*I envy the moonshine in your hair,*
*I envy the starlight on your body,*
*Your love is my wound's remedy…*
*I wonder, do you hear me, dear?*

Sitting on the rock, Spyros was writing in his notebook. Only that way, could he find an outlet for his pain.

He had a faint hope that Marisol would give him a second chance.

He loved her, he adored her, he felt half without her.

It seems that the heavens were open…

"Marisol!" he shouted when he saw her going down the strait to the sea.

The girl stood short.

"How long will you be avoiding me, my heart?" he pleaded as he approached her. "How long? Don't you see how much… how much…"

Marisol looked at him, in tears.

*I envy the moonshine in your hair,*
*I envy the starlight on your body,*
*Your love is my wound's remedy…*
*I wonder, do you hear me, dear?*

Spyros whispered in her ear, hugging her.

Marisol slightly pushed him away.

"I loved you very much… and I still love you… and I neither can nor want to take you out of my heart. I don't want your jealousy! I want your love and trust! I never gave you the right to doubt me!"

"I go crazy… I go crazy when I think…"

"I never gave you the right to doubt me!" she repeated, stressing the words one by one. "I want your love and trust! But if you can't do that, then…"

Spyros began to tremble.

"I want you… I love you… so much that… that I would take you and go away to a desert island, just the two of us… so that no one can see us… so that no one ever separate us… only death. Do you hear me? Only death!"

He pressed her tight against him and started kissing her voraciously.

"You're hurting me… you're hurting me," she said chokingly.

In her attempt to get rid of this suffocating hug, she stumbled, lost her balance, and fell on the rocky ground.

"Marisol!" shouted Spyros. "Marisol!"

No answer… no movement, not even a slight one.

A thin line of blood had begun to form on the back of her head.

****

"Mary of Fire… Mary of Temptation… Mary of Sin…" he heard the sick man muttering.

He shook his hand hard.

The sick man made a superhuman effort and sat up.

"That woman… didn't let me rest… my body, my mind, my being… I longed for her and hated her… I hated her and longed for her… and I hated you too, because you had her… and I hated myself, because… because…" a loud dry cough made him shake all over.

"She was a… a prostitute…" he continued. "I saw… I saw how the other men looked at her… and you were jealous… you were dying… and I… I was glad that you no longer had her… Marisol… She was not the Mary of the Sun… no… no…. She was a hellfire…! That afternoon, I saw you… I saw how you begged her to take you back… I saw your despair… I saw you go off like a dog… when…"

*I was the killer… yes… even if I didn't mean to… I…*, thought Brother Raphael, trying to hold back his tears.

"I approached her… and then… then I saw her wiggle and slightly move her lips. She was desirable… desirable even in that state!

The lava… the lava flared up… it sought a way out… no… I shouldn't… I put my hand on her nose and mouth… and… it only lasted a little… very little… then… silence!"

Brother Raphael jumped up.

"My God! My God!" he shouted. "Why? Why, Alexis, why?"

He grabbed the sick man by the shoulders and started shaking him.

"How could you live with this secret? How?"

He had spent fifteen whole years in tears, prayer, remorse for a crime he had never committed. For fifteen whole years, he lived in a lie, the biggest lie.

"I left everything… I lost everything… my job… my life… Marisol… this is all I have left… only this…"

He opened the upper part of his cassock, revealing to Alexis the ring with the rose hanging from the chain. "How could you? How could you?"

"I could… but…"

A strong convulsion shook him.

Then he remained motionless.

With a trembling hand, Brother Raphael closed the dead man's eyes.

"May He forgive you," he said. "But I… I… cannot…"

He opened the door of the room.

He only said, "It's over!"

And he left in the night.

The dawn found him at the cemetery, where his beloved Marisol rested.

*When the sea was filled with blood,*

*The roses stopped blooming…*

*Only one was left…*

*A mark on the finger and the heart…*

he murmured.

He sent a kiss to the photo that looked at him smiling.

"I love you! I will always love you," he declared.

"Live…!" her adored voice caressed him like a gentle breeze. "Live, my love!"

# *Part Four*
### *When the night smells of iris and jasmine,*
### *it's my love that will come knocking on your window.*

### *The Ribbons of Revenge*

1

*I sit and reminisce about those beautiful August days, what if the wave took them away and destroyed them? And since then, I hated you. But − how ironic! − I came here to quietly spend as much time as my writing has in store for me and every day I see you through my window. Sometimes, you're calm, sometimes stormy and you always change colours: deep blue, turquoise, green, angry grey. You remind me… Oh, how much you remind me of!*

The intense cough that frequently tormented him of late cut his daydreaming short.

"You will uproot my breast!" he shouted angrily.

He wiped his mouth and nose with a tissue. His gaze fell on the mirror across from him.

"We are growing old… growing old," he monologued.

He opened the first drawer of his nightstand and pulled out a faded box, slightly frayed at the edges.

*My secret and little friend*, he thought. *I sealed you… then… but now's the time… to…*

*Ah… the letter… the red dress… the sea…*

In him, nothing had gone blurry!

2

The older the photo, the stronger the emotions it conjures up. It reminds us of our dreams and how we thought we had all the time in the world to make them come true, the life that passes, the repressed frustrations and the "ah's!" we never found the strength to look straight in the eye.

Her laughter was so sweet but also so loud that it "pierced" the slightly yellowed printed paper and echoed in his ears. The water reached up to her waist. Her hair was tied with a red ribbon. Half-wet tufts escaped and fell on her cheeks. And with a jump, sometimes she was lost at the bottom and other times she rose back to the surface.

"Mermaid!" he hollered at her. "Crazy little mermaid!"

"The sea is my destiny!" she'd say over and over.

A tear escaped from the corner of his eye and rolled down his cheek, then another… and another.

*So, you can still cry,* he thought. *Not all your tears have turned to stone, as you feared…*

"Ariadne!" he whispered.

Here's another photo. The girl of the sea, Ariadne, hugging *him!*

"He… the one who…" he monologued.

*"She's both fire and saltiness… her body… her smell… they turn me on… they drive me crazy… I long for her, dude, like crazy… I lose my mind when…" he said.*

*"I see it in her eyes, how much she loves you…"*

*"I too melt from craziness over her… passion…"*

*"She's sensitive; don't you get it? You fool! Since you don't love her, why do you give her false hopes? Let her go… then… then, it may be too late…"*

*"And why do you care?"*

Sometimes, true love is hidden in the silence, and when the night falls, it wanders alone, looking for answers, or tries to be redeemed by carving words on a piece of paper.

3

It was getting dark.

Slowly a full moon began to emerge over the waves. And it went up… and up… and up… until it took its place in the sky.

He lit the lamp next to him and put on his glasses.

The moonlight coming in from the grilles formed strange shapes, giving him the feeling that shadows were hovering around him, keeping him company. This probably relieved him, because he sought them in his loneliness, no matter how much he insisted that he had come to terms with it.

*It's time,* he thought.

He dragged his fingers on the surface of the box, opened it, and sniffed it, letting the thin layer of dust penetrate deep into his entrails like an at the same time hot and cool breath.

Everything was there… as if not a day had passed…

For some inexplicable reason, he kept in a forgotten case in his wallet only the photos that showed the sea girl playing with the waves and hugging *him!*

The journey was about to begin…

Now, the shadows got flesh, blood, and names…

4

*Once upon a time, there was a girl named Ariadne. But unlike her namesake princess, she threw the thread into the sea, from the moment that he entered her life… even now, I find it hard to say his name! She found herself in a maze from which she couldn't – or didn't want to? – get out. She probably got out, but in a way that's…*

*BUT LET ME NOT GET AHEAD OF MYSELF, EH!* He put the brakes on his thought.

He held in his hands the hardcover notebook with the embossed decoration: a red rose on the cover… and on the back, a composition of honeysuckle, iris and jasmine.

On the front page, a glued photo showed all three of them smiling, in some carefree moment in time.

*Years of our youth…! We thought that you would last forever!* he thought.

*Fire… saltiness… passion… craze… her body… her smell… I crave her…* the words of that guy – whose name he couldn't even bear to say! – danced in his mind.

And there they were… her soul, her poems unfolded in the following pages.

He could see the outline of a shadow materialising on the wall. "You never understood! You fool… or rather not fool but… criminal!" he shouted and shut his eyes wide, as if he wanted to exorcise that invisible presence, which for some reason he seemed to hate to death.

When he reopened them, the shadow had disappeared.

He took a deep breath.

"You were so beautiful… your face… your physique… your gaze… and above all your heart… and your thinking, my dear!" he said softly. "Why? Why didn't you understand? Why? Why?"

He had to find the strength and say *his* name. He had to… He had to…

*Once upon a time, there were two friends… Angelos and Avgoustis…*

5

Today and yesterday are mixed together, breaking the barrier of time.

With a blurred look, he tried to distinguish the torrent from words and emotions.

*The lyrics I once wrote,*
*I wrote them to show you my love,*
*but you didn't see, you didn't hear, you didn't feel…*

He closed the notebook abruptly.

Every page, every word was a memory.

"You didn't deserve it! You didn't deserve it!" he shouted.

****

*Flame… passion… what can they have in common with love? They burn, they plunder, they pillage… and then, you mourn over the ashes…!* he thought, looking at the once happy mermaid girl with black circles around her eyes, without her bright smile.

After raising her to the stars, *he* then knocked her down to the ground abruptly. A strong fall, without end.

And as time passed, her torment grew.

Until…

****

"Remember it… remember it all…" he almost ordered himself.

But… how could he forget in the first place? He had locked everything up in a corner of his mind… and…

6

Silently, she looked at the horizon. She hoped that time would alleviate her sorrow and frustration. Yet, the opposite was happening. Her heart was deadened.

She let her clothes fall on the pebbles and dived in the sea. How peaceful it was! The sun had begun to set in the west, leaving its reflection on the water's surface. And she was moving… moving… moving, as if pushed by an invisible hand.

"Come… come…" she felt a voice inviting her.

"How beautiful I feel! Don't… don't leave me… hold me…" she said in a low voice.

The water slowly covered her back, her shoulders, her hair.

She let herself go.

The *little mermaid* returned where she belonged.

****

His hands trembled as he opened the envelope. And those words!

*"I close my eyes and walk naked… in a blue that has no end. I can't leave this hug; I don't have the strength to do so. From now on, I won't cry alone, I won't be alone. In the blast of the wind, in the light of the moon, in the play of the waves, I will sing about love, visible and invisible at the same time, for you! Free from pain and tears, I will be able to worship you to infinity….!"*

A little further on, a fire-red dress was forgotten, alone and orphaned by her body and her existence.

7

He kissed the yellowed paper. On the edge, the letters were slightly blurry with tears.

"I don't want to remember; I don't want to!" he insisted.

How he wished it were all just a dream. But…

****

Next day's dusk found Angelos sitting in the same place – where the woe happened! – tightly clutching her dress to his chest. He was speechless, his face deadpan. Next to him, his friend Avgoustis was shaking with sobs.

"It's your fault!" he cried.

"My fault?"

"Yes, it was you… you…! You never loved her… you never listened to her heart… to truly see…! You… you used her in the most disgraceful way!

You killed her! You became an angel of death… you…"

He snatched the dress from Angelos' hands.

"Only I could see her tears. She tried to hide from me, but she didn't succeed. Where were you, huh? Where were you? And now you dare to hold her dress in your hands! Don't defile it… don't…"

The last moments passed in front of him like a movie.

*"I'm going to get some air; I'm suffocating in here…"*
*"Let me come with you, dear…"*
*She smiled sadly.*
*"Only you love me, only you feel me, my heart," she told him and kissed him on the forehead.*
*How encouraged he was with her kiss!*
*He was about to follow her, but she didn't want him to.*
*"I will come again…" she whispered and shook his hand tenderly.*

"Farewell… farewell…"

"What did you say? Angelos asked him.

"You didn't deserve such a woman… no… no… you didn't deserve her! Oh, my God, how can I accept that this beauty, this creature was swallowed by the sea? How???"

Angelos bowed his head, and a loud groan came out of his chest.

At *"their"* emerald beach, with the rocks and the caves, where their sharp, passionate breaths still resounded as they came together with the "I love you's!" that she mentally whispered to him… that was where she had chosen to write the end in her own way.

8

Her absence already haunted him. Remorse, along with Avgoustis' angry words, began to open his eyes and make him realise how foolishly, how criminally he had behaved. He would never find love like that woman's again.

He took her photo out of his pocket, kissed it, and cried.

Yes, this rational, this so cerebral guy cried!

"Stop…!!! Only I… only I have the right to cry… me… who loved her like a Virgin Mary…! Don't cry… stop… stop… stop…" Avgoustis shouted at him.

Torn, Angelos fell in his friend's arms.

"I'm sorry…! I'm sorry!" he stuttered.

He was grasped on him as if he were his only refuge.

"It's getting dark…" he repeated once he calmed down a bit. "All I have now… is this letter… and…"

"I… I will have something more… her last kiss…" claimed Avgoustis.

He touched his forehead.

*When the night smells of iris and jasmine, it's my love that will come knocking on your window…* he whispered.

"I don't… I don't…" Angelos hesitated.

"Just for me, Ariadne, my soul, just for me…"

Angelos lowered his gaze in shame.

However…

"Yours was her kiss just before the end… and her beautiful words… those were yours too… I'd say… that you won…!"

"Apparently, nothing touches you!" said Avgoustis, casting a murderous look that mirrored all the hatred that was beginning to be born in him for someone he once considered a friend and a brother.

Only for one moment.

Then his gaze turned again in pain to the sea as if he were looking from it to bring back to him what he had loved and longed for more in his life.

"She let herself in sea waves… she left… but she's here… she lives in here," he whispered, putting her hand on her heart.

"You… you've been dead for a long time!" he continued in an icy voice.

He stood up, still holding the dress in his arms.

"Whoever stays near you loses their soul, Angelos!"

Angelos was about to say something, but Avgoustis cut him off, raising his hand, without looking at him.

"There is nothing left…! Go…!"

"But…"

"Go away, then… go… go… go!" Avgoustis' voice dripped with both pain and rage.

9

Angelos left crushed with heavy steps. He felt that he had no air in his lungs. And how could he, anyway? Guilt… it held a tight noose around his neck. Impossible to untie the knot. A bloody tear dripped on the place for his heart, but it was vacant, so it had nowhere to stand. Thus, he continued his course following the dark and icy path of his soul.

He was walking with his head down. He felt a dark figure in front of him and raised his eyes. A hooded man was leading him, pulling him by a chain… Angelos was shaken by surprise.

"What is it, Angelos?" he heard a hollow voice. "Don't you recognise me? I'm Fear. Did you think that I don't exist?"

He had lost his speech. Either way, would he ever need it again? To do what with it? To ask what *"Where am I going?"* He knew already. To Doom.

There was nothing left for him.

Ariadne had ended her life because of him, because he had taken advantage of her. An innocent soul who really loved him! And along with her, he had lost Avgoustis too… Avgoustis, who had been a friend and a brother.

It made no sense for him to think. After all, think about what? The road had no return.

And suddenly…

"But how?" he stammered. "How did I find myself in the damned cave?"

Its interior was huge and dark. All around, there was an eerie silence.

Trying to get his eyes used to the dark… he thought he saw a glow. He walked carefully towards the bright place.

"Is anybody there?" he shouted, and his echo sent his own voice in response.

He felt a hot breath back on his neck and made a move to turn around, surprised. He didn't complete it. A darkness even thicker than that inside the cave enveloped him, and he fell to the ground… he only saw with the corner of his eye his senses turn their back on him and leave.

When he came round, the darkness was just as dense. He got up stumbling and hit something metallic. He leaned back, holding his head where it had hit, and his back rested on the same surface. Trembling with fear, he turned around like crazy, round and round to find a way out.

But…

"It's vain, Angelos," he heard a wooden voice. "You're in an iron cage. So, don't rush to leave."

"Who are you?" he asked, terrified.

"The one who will judge and condemn you. Or rather… to put it more correctly… the one who judged and condemned you. The trial has taken place, and the decision has been made. Can you guess it? Don't, you don't need to. I do not wish to tire your stupid head anymore! The decision is… Death, Angelos. Tough and relentless. Vindictive Death. Vengeful Death. Death god, Angelos."

Angelos listened, bathed in sweat. For the first time in his life, he felt paralysed, losing control. He tried to focus on the voice. It reminded him of something. But what?

"Who are you?" the ridiculous question came again.

"Your worst nightmare…"

And then…

A flame began to flicker and illuminate the room a little. Angelos saw a red ribbon burning, tied to one edge of the cage. He tried to distinguish the figure, but it moved in the opposite direction. Soon, another red ribbon appeared, burning on the other side of the cage… then another… and another.

Soon, the entire cage became a burning prison… red ribbons were burning, suffocating him with smokes.

Only when the fire lit up the whole cave, did Angelos manage to see the figure that led him to a burning, suffocating death.

"You?" he asked panting.

"The answer, Angelos, is… Only me. It couldn't be anyone else. Only me."

"I'm suffocating…" Angelos's voice came out lifeless.

"Correct. You *are* suffocating. But not from the smoke. That's not the end I saved for you…"

Angelos saw the ribbon in his hands and understood, just one moment before it was wrapped around his neck, taking his last breath.

10

Back at sea, Avgoustis' aching gaze hadn't found closure… maybe because the sea refused his vows and didn't bring back his beloved.

Before seeing the shine, he felt the warmth behind him.

"Ariadne…" he whispered.

"Avgoustis," he heard her sweet voice behind his back.

He didn't turn around. He didn't want the dream to end.

"Come back, Avgoustis, and… and forgive me…" he heard her begging again.

He turned around very slowly, as if slowing down his movement would capture the moment and turn it into reality.

"Open your eyes, Avgoustis. I'm here…"

He opened them slowly. He thought he saw Ariadne as a white vision, but he wasn't sure, because the hot tears had blurred his vision.

"Forgive me…"

She was indeed there, in front of him.

"For what, my dear? What did you do wrong to ask me to forgive you?"

"I couldn't understand… I couldn't see… I'm sorry."

"Why did you leave, Ariadne?" he asked, choking a sob with effort. "Why? How am I supposed to live without you?"

"You'll live, my dear. You have to live and move on. You have to love again."

"No matter how many lives I live, I will love you again, Ariadne. It's you I will be waiting to meet again."

The light enveloped him and reached the depths of his soul, as she looked at him with infinite love now. Her figure began to fade, to disappear, leaving behind a thin line of stardust.

"When it's time, I will come to you, Ariadne," he swore to her.


For a moment, he stood motionless looking at the place where she – until just a second ago! – was standing. Then he turned toward the sea again.

"You took her from me. So, now take this from me, and I'm done with you," he stated, scattering burnt red strips of cloth to be picked up by the waves.


****


*What could be left now?*
*A journal with leaves yellowed over time,*
*A photograph, a little worn in the corners,*

*It doesn't speak… but it looks you deep in the eyes,*
*And a dried rose*
*Forgotten in a wooden box…*
read Avgoustis.

Her words found their way to his heart again. *AND SINCE THEN, EVERY AUGUST, I'VE BEEN IN PAIN,* he wrote on a page of the notebook in capital letters.

He wrapped a red ribbon with blackened tips around his fingers a couple of times and brought it to his lips.

*"When it's time, I will come to you, Ariadne!"* The words of that oath came back to his mind.

His body began to relax… his eyelids were sealed… he surrendered in a world of eternal dream.

Next to a deep blue sea, Ariadne was waiting for him, reaching out her hand.

"You came!" she only said.

He hugged her and held her tight.

"Do you remember…? *No matter how many lives I live, I will always carry you in me… It's you I will be waiting to meet again…"* he said, filling her beautiful face with kisses.

Behind the rocks, a grey melancholic shadow, dissonance in the bright landscape, sighed heavily. Doomed to wander forever without being able to find peace, it had now been forgotten by all.

# Part Five
## The Lyrics of My Heart...

### Silence

1

The hours of my silence scream
Words that were never said
And truths that were closed in a mirror.
The hours of my silence scream
For what I didn't get to live
And for what I kept locked
In a secret nook of my heart.
The hours of my silence scream
For a dream that faded,
For the rain that soaked my insides,
For the tear that was left hanging
At the corner of my eyes.
The hours of my silence scream.
Is anybody listening?

2

Longings travel
On the liquid blue veil.
Lost dreams walk
On the rails of some train.
The sea turned stormy.
Will you moor, my love, at a shelter?
Fog rolled in.
The "I love you's" that stayed hidden in us,
Will they find the way?
Silence, my consolation and lover,
What sea god enchanted you?
My big, vast silence,
In which station did you get off and left?
Time passed,
Night advanced,
But I'm here, waiting for you,
In the wind, and at sea,
On earth, and in the sky.

### Rain

I'm not scared of the dark,
I've been dressed in night for a long time now.
I'm not scared of the rain,
It's my bosom friend and frees me
From what still hurts me.
Don't ask me why I love the rain,
Let me just pick up its drops with a kiss,
And hang them around my neck as an amulet,
To remember.
I'm waiting for a rainbow to appear…
Your eyes.
I'm here,
Though the hours pass in the sphere of eternity…
Lost moments…
If you follow the path of the rain,
You will find me again.
But hurry,
Come before it's too late, and time stops.


### Anticipation

The old mansions,
Alone and deserted by the port,
How many moments they reminisce and cry!
The bougainvillea well up, withered in their garden,
And these salt-worn windows keep shedding tears.
Who said that the lifeless don't have a soul?
If they could talk, they'd tell us so much…
Stories that froze over time,
Loves and romances that were forgotten.
Tonight, the sea found its calm,
The sky was filled with a thousand colours,
Loneliness was dressed in deep blue, and it smelled saltiness.
In the vastness of silence,
A key seemed to creak in the rusty door.
I wonder, is it true, or just another fallacy?

### *Let There Be Light*

Let there be light.
I took off the night attire from my shoulders,
And put on the sea.
Let there be light.
Flowers sprouted on the twigs.
Red and white
Like the soul's sacred passions.
Let there be light.
The sun is my friend and brother.
Endless blue.
Life.

## THE END